DINOSAUR DAYS

WRITTEN BY **LINDA MANNING**

PICTURES BY **VLASTA VAN KAMPEN**

Troll Medallion

Library of Congress Cataloging-in-Publication Data
Manning, Linda, (date)
Dinosaur days / by Linda Manning; pictures by Vlasta van Kampen.
p.   cm.
Summary: Each day of the week a different dinosaur appears
at a girl's house to engage in some kind of mischief.
ISBN 0-8167-3315-5 (lib.)   ISBN 0-8167-3316-3 (pbk.)
[1. Dinosaurs–Fiction.   2. Days –Fiction.   3. Stories in rhyme.]
I. Van Kampen, Vlasta, ill.   II. Title.
PZ8.3.M3557Di   1994
[E]–dc20   93-28443

Published by Troll Associates, Inc.

First published in 1993 by
Stoddart Publishing Co., Limited
34 Lesmill Road
Toronto, Canada
M3B 2T6

First published in the United States by BridgeWater Books.

Printed in the United States of America.

10   9   8   7   6   5   4   3   2   1

For David, who loved dinosaurs.

— Linda

*For a little village kid who discovered dinosaurs
in the big city museum — my brother, Vic.*

— Vlasta

What if on Monday
A pudgy green dinosaur

Slipped from the cupboard
Slurped up your orange juice and
Squished flat your toast . . .

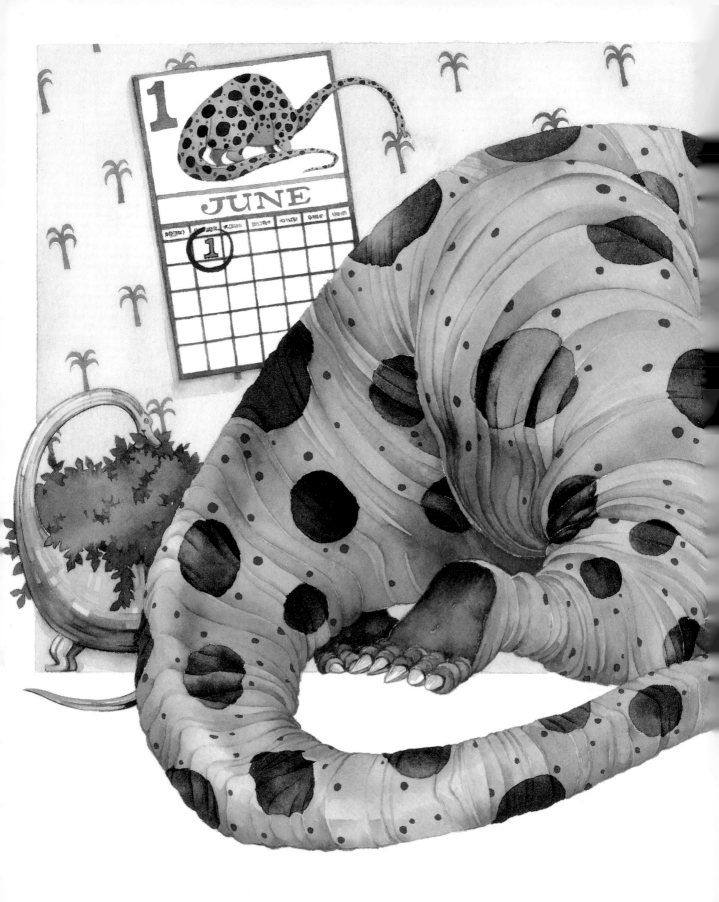

Would you tame him and teach him to lie by a post?

What if on Tuesday
A strange scaley dinosaur

Popped from your closet
Drew on your ceiling
And messed up your clothes . . .

Would you catch her and hold her by two ticklish toes?

What if on Wednesday
A wet muddy dinosaur

Roared through the garden
Left tracks on the curtains
And jumped on a chair . . .

Would you dry his spikes quickly, or slowly, with care?

What if on Thursday
A shy smiling dinosaur

Slid from the drain pipe
Scratched up some pansies and
Ate your prize rose . . .

Would you teach her to skip with an old piece of hose?

What if on Friday
A divebombing dinosaur

Crashed through the ceiling
And squished gooey toothpaste
All over the wall . . .

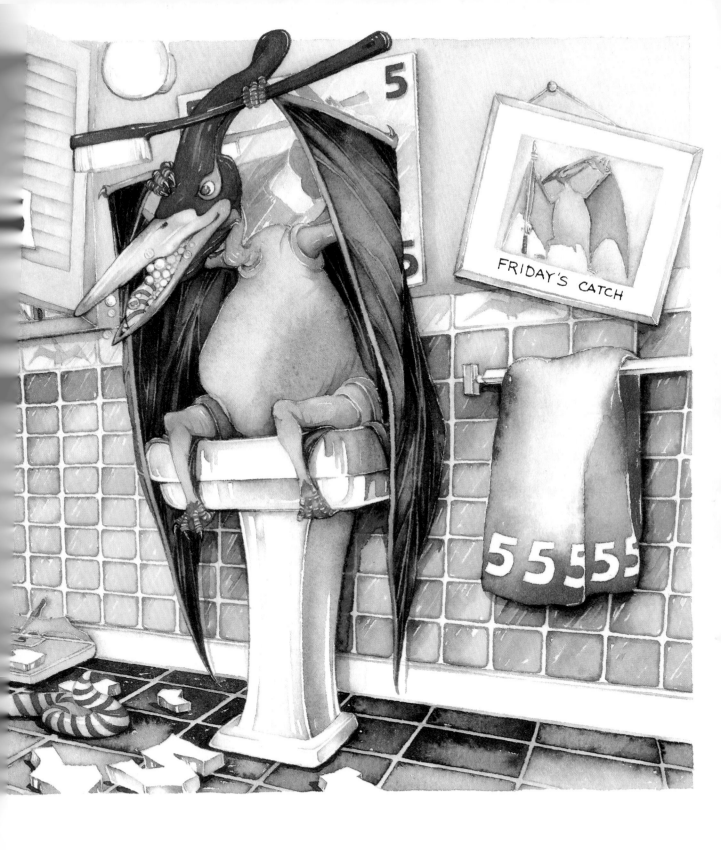

Would you teach him his name in dinosaur scrawl?

What if on Saturday
A rude rumbling dinosaur

Rolled from the dryer
Spilled the detergent
And plugged up the drain . . .

Would you say quite severely, "Don't do that again"?

What if on Sunday
A fancy chef dinosaur
Took over your yard

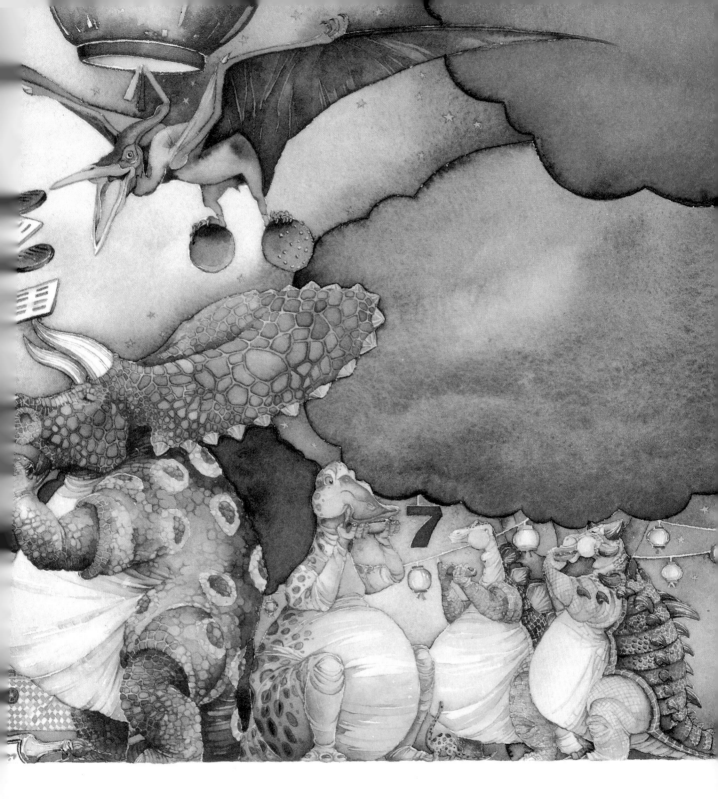

To cook hot dogs and burgers
All sizzling and popping
With ketchup and toppings . . .
Would you let all the dinosaurs gather around
To guzzle and gulp till their tummies were round?

What a week it has been!
A pudgy green dinosaur slipped in on Monday
A strange scaley dinosaur popped in on Tuesday
A wet muddy dinosaur roared in on Wednesday
A shy smiling dinosaur slid down on Thursday
A divebombing dinosaur crashed in on Friday
A rude rumbling dinosaur rolled in on Saturday . . .

Then all of the dinosaurs
sprawled in a heap
And fell sound asleep
On Sunday!

Dinosaur Glossary

MONDAY

Apatosaurus (a-pat-o-*sore*-us) — the largest of the dinosaurs, weighing as much as thirteen elephants; plant-eating.

TUESDAY
Stegosaurus (steg-uh-*sore*-us) — a large dinosaur with a double row of plates along its back and large, powerful tail; plant-eating.

WEDNESDAY

Ankylosaurus (an-keel-o-*sore*-us) — a dinosaur with spikes sticking out on either side of its back; plant-eating.

THURSDAY
Hadrosaurus (had-ro-*sore*-us) — a duck-billed dinosaur; plant-eating.

FRIDAY

Pteranodon (ter-*an*-o-don) — flying dinosaur, with very large wings; for food, this dinosaur scooped up fish as it flew.

SATURDAY

Triceratops (try-*sair*-ah-tops) — a dinosaur with three horns on its head; plant-eating.

SUNDAY
Tyrannosaurus Rex (tie-ran-uh-*sore*-us rex) — largest and fiercest meat-eating dinosaur.